PEDRO AND THE MONKEY

PEDRO AND THE MONKEY

RETOLD FROM FILIPINO FOLKLORE BY
ROBERT D. SAN SOUCI

ILLUSTRATED BY
MICHAEL HAYS

MORROW JUNIOR BOOKS
New York

Acrylic on linen was used for the full-color illustrations.
The text type is 13-point Bookman Lt. BT.

Text copyright © 1996 by Robert D. San Souci
Illustrations copyright © 1996 by Michael Hays

Printed in Hong Kong by South China Printing Company (1988) Ltd.

1 2 3 4 5 6 7 8 9 10

Library of Congress Cataloging-in-Publication Data
San Souci, Robert D.
Pedro and the monkey / retold from Filipino folklore [by] Robert D. San Souci; illustrated by Michael Hays.
p. cm.
Includes bibliographical references.
Summary: A sly monkey secures the fortune of his young owner in this variation of a traditional Filipino tale.
ISBN 0-688-13743-1 (trade)—ISBN 0-688-13744-X (library)
[1. Folklore—Philippines. 2. Monkeys—Folklore.] I. Hays, Michael, ill. II. Title.
PZ8.1.S227Pe 1996   398.2'09599'02—dc20   95-35385   CIP AC

To Erin, Ford, and Wesley—
Thanks for being such wonderful friends!
—R.S.S.

For Danny, Katie, and Sarah
—M.H.

Long ago, Pedro, a young Filipino farmer, was plagued by a monkey who stole corn from his field. Finally the young man set a snare for the thief.

The next day, he found the monkey caught in the trap. "I'm going to sell you to someone as a pet!" said Pedro. "That will repay me for all the corn you've stolen."

The monkey burst into tears. Then, to Pedro's amazement, the monkey begged, "Please let me go. I promise not to steal any more corn."

Pedro had a generous heart, so he set the creature free.

Now the monkey said, "In return for your kindness, I will arrange for you to marry the daughter of Don Francisco, the rich landowner."

"What nonsense," said Pedro, chuckling, "since I am so poor. Can you change that?"

"Wait and see!" cried the monkey. Then he scampered off to the grand manor of Don Francisco.

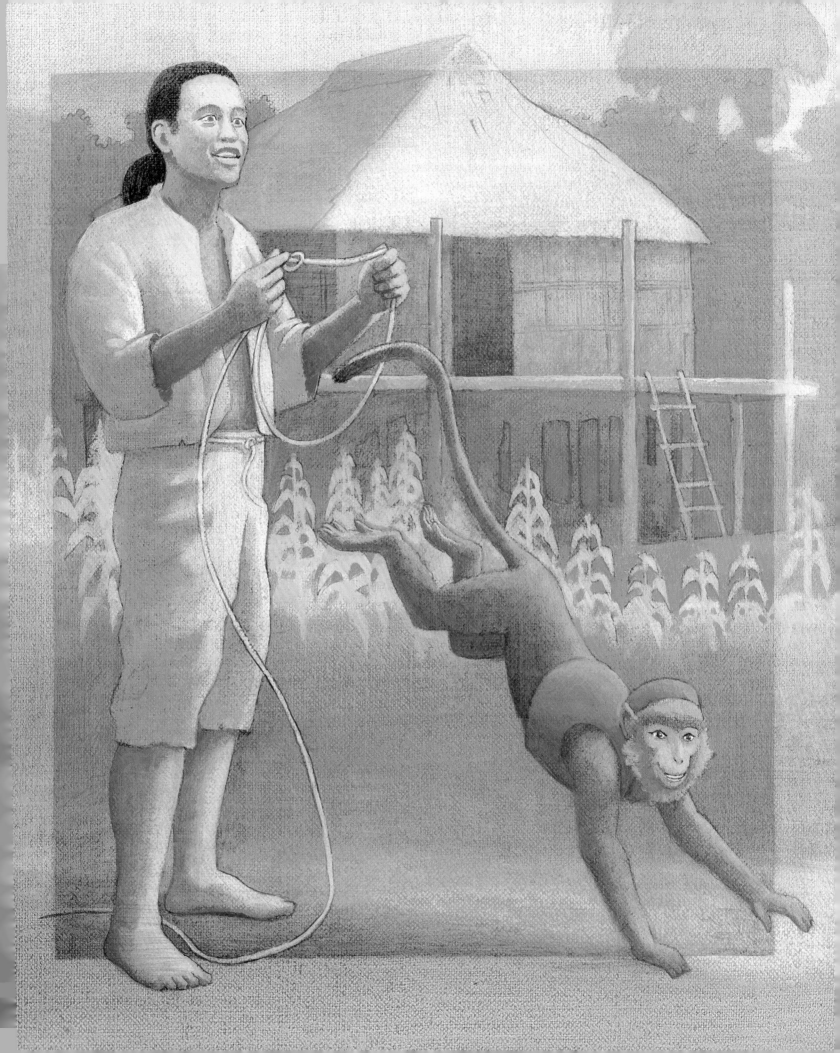

He found the wealthy man seated in the shade of an old *bubog* tree, its branches spread like an umbrella. Bowing low, the monkey said, "Sir, my master, Don Pedro, graciously asks to borrow your *ganta*-measure, so that he may tally up his money."

Charmed by the monkey's good manners, Don Francisco handed him the square wooden box he used to measure out rice.

When the monkey scurried back to Pedro's farm, the young man asked, "Why did you bring me a *ganta*? I don't have enough rice to fill it even once."

"This has nothing to do with what you have, but with what will come to you," the monkey said mysteriously. "Now, loan me three *centavos*."

"That is all the money I have!" said Pedro. But he gave the monkey the coins anyway.

The next morning, the monkey stuck Pedro's three *centavos* to the inside of the measure before he returned it.

When Don Francisco saw the coins, he held them out to the monkey, saying, "These belong to your master."

"Oh," said the monkey, laughing, "three *centavos* don't mean anything to someone as rich as Don Pedro. Please keep them to pay for the loan of your *ganta*-measure."

And off he went, leaving Don Francisco astounded to think there was someone living nearby who might be richer than he.

When the monkey told Pedro what had happened, the farmer complained, "First you eat my corn. Now you give away my money. If I was not so poor already, I would say you have ruined me."

"Have patience," said the monkey. "You'll be rewarded soon enough."

One week later, the monkey presented himself at Don Francisco's door. Bowing low, he said, "My master, Don Pedro, wishes to borrow your *ganta*-measure again. He has just made a great deal more money and wants to measure it."

"Who is this master of yours who *measures* his coins, while I *count* mine?" asked Don Francisco.

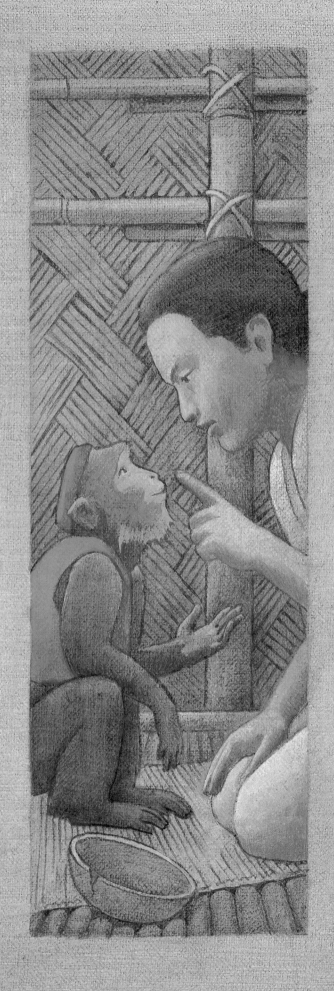

"Why, he is the richest man in the world!" said the monkey. "But he is shy and rarely leaves his house."

Don Francisco went to fetch the measure. But before he gave it to the monkey, he stuck four gold coins to the bottom. "Now we'll find out who's the richer man!" he said to himself.

When Pedro saw the coins, he exclaimed, "Return these at once! Don Francisco will think we have stolen them!"

"Don't worry," the monkey insisted. "This shows how well my plan is going."

The next morning, the monkey returned the measure, leaving the gold coins untouched. Don Francisco made a great show of discovering them. "Do these belong to your master?" he asked.

The monkey chuckled and said, "My master is getting careless. But it's only money—keep it. These days Don Pedro is more concerned with finding a wife."

Thinking that a man wealthy enough to be indifferent to gold would be an ideal son-in-law, Don Francisco said, "I have a daughter, Maria. Perhaps your master will dine with us tomorrow, and we can all become better acquainted."

"Don Pedro will be delighted," the monkey assured him.

When the monkey told Pedro what had happened, the farmer said, "How can I call on Don Francisco and Maria? They will know I'm a poor man the moment they see my shabby clothes."

"Leave that to me," said the monkey. Then he hurried to the shop of the clothes merchant.

"My master, Don Pedro, the richest man in the world, desires a new outfit," said the monkey. "He asks that you put the charge on his account, and he will pay you within the month."

"Of course," the merchant replied, pleased to have such a wealthy customer.

So it was that Pedro and the monkey went to dine with Don Francisco and Maria.

The moment they met, Pedro and Maria found themselves charmed by each other's company. All during the meal, they could not keep their eyes off each other. By evening's end, they had fallen in love.

When he was about to leave, Pedro, carried away with emotion, said to Don Francisco, "If Maria agrees, and if it pleases you, I would like to marry her."

"Oh, yes!" cried Maria.

But all Don Francisco said was, "Perhaps you will invite us to your house, and we can discuss this matter further."

Realizing that he could not invite them to his poor farmhouse, Pedro said nothing. But the monkey spoke right up. "My master is embarrassed because he is having some rooms added to his manor and the house is unfit for guests. However, the work is nearly done. In three days, I will escort you to Don Pedro's estate."

Astonished by what the monkey said, Pedro only nodded. But after they departed, he asked, "How can I entertain Maria and her father in my hut? It is impossible!"

"Not long ago, you believed it was impossible to dine at Don Francisco's table," replied the monkey. "Just leave things to me."

Early the next morning, the monkey roused Pedro from his bed. "Fetch a length of rope, an axhead, and a drum, then come with me."

"Where are we going?" asked Pedro.

"To the giant, Burincantada."

"Burincantada is a monster!" cried Pedro. "He eats all the people he catches."

"He is also a fool and a coward," answered the monkey. "If you hope to marry Maria, you'll do as I say."

So Pedro gathered everything the monkey told him to. Then they followed an old road that led through the jungle to the giant's house high on a hill.

Burincantada's manor was very grand—far too elegant for such a creature. In fact, he had gobbled up the rightful owners long ago.

"You stay hidden," the monkey told Pedro. "When I signal, pound the drum loudly." Then, carrying the rope and the metal axhead, the monkey boldly knocked on the giant's huge door.

With a growl, Burincantada wrenched the door open. He was so hideous, with blazing red eyes and curving tusks, that the monkey had to summon all his courage to keep from running away.

"What do you want?" the giant roared.

"Sir," said the monkey, "a huge, horrible ogre is coming this way. He is eating every living thing he finds. I know you have deep caves under your house. Please let me hide there."

This news frightened the cowardly giant, but he blustered, "Why should I be afraid? I'm a giant, too!"

"Truly a *giant* among giants," the monkey said flatteringly. "But this ogre stands ten times as tall as you. He has six heads, and each of his six mouths is filled with three rows of metal teeth. I myself have seen him snatch up a handful of *carabao* and swallow these water buffalo down in a single bite. But he has a special liking for giants; that's why he is called the Giant-Eater."

"Oh, oh, oh!" wailed Burincantada. "Can such a monster really exist?"

"Look," said the monkey, letting the length of rope dangle from his paw. "As proof of what I'm saying, I brought a hair from the ogre's head."

Next he held up the axhead, saying, "This tiny tooth broke off when he was chewing stones to sharpen his teeth."

Finally the monkey signaled Pedro, who began pounding on the drum. "Hear that booming?" yelled the monkey. "The Giant-Eater is beating his chest to challenge you. He's almost here!"

"I must hide!" wailed Burincantada. He ran to a huge trapdoor, lifted it, and plunged down a flight of steps that led deep into the mountain.

Quickly the monkey slammed the trapdoor shut. When Pedro joined him, the two of them sealed it with an iron bar.

Searching the house, they found one room filled with gold, while another room held cages crowded with people. Pedro and the monkey freed the captives, who promised to do anything to help their rescuers.

Pedro set half of them to cleaning the house and the other half to tending the cattle and plowing the fields of the estate. The monkey told them, "If anyone asks who owns all this, say that everything belongs to Don Pedro."

Two days later, the monkey escorted Don Francisco and Maria to the grand house where Pedro now lived. As Don Francisco's carriage passed the herdsmen and field hands, the rich man asked, "Whose cattle and lands are these?"

The men answered, "They belong to our master, Don Pedro."

Finally the carriage came to a stop in front of the magnificent house on the hill. There Pedro, looking every inch the richest man in the world, greeted his guests.

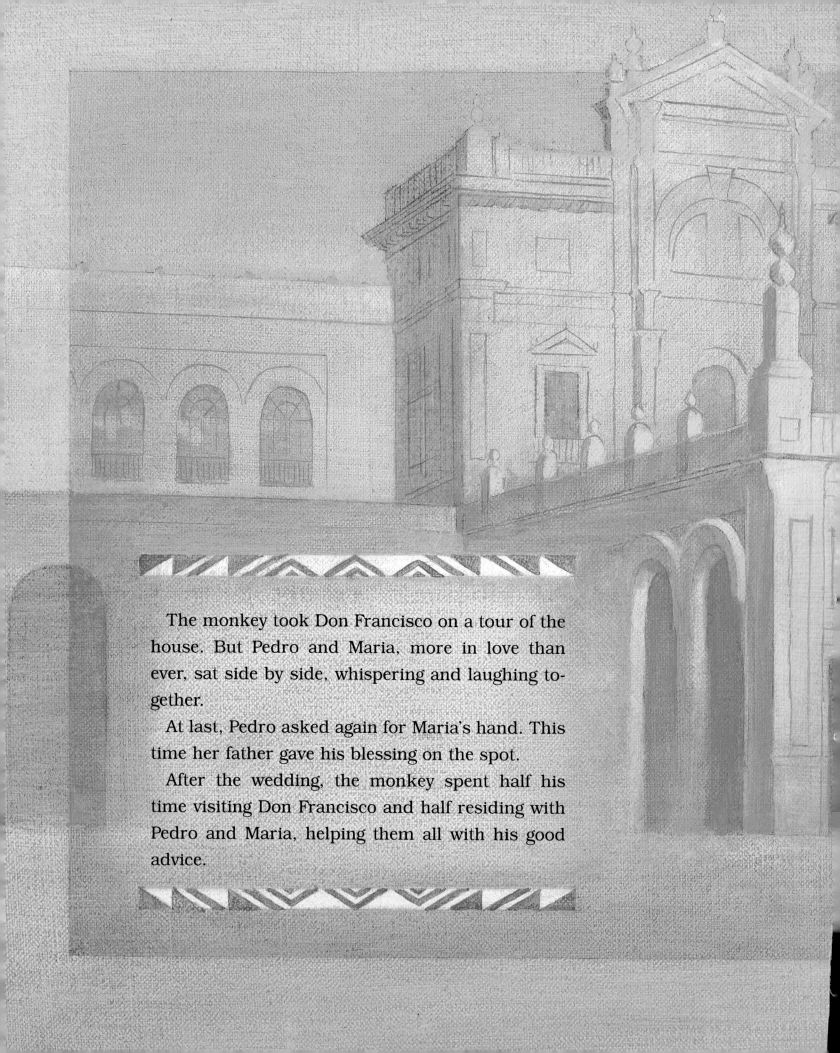

The monkey took Don Francisco on a tour of the house. But Pedro and Maria, more in love than ever, sat side by side, whispering and laughing together.

At last, Pedro asked again for Maria's hand. This time her father gave his blessing on the spot.

After the wedding, the monkey spent half his time visiting Don Francisco and half residing with Pedro and Maria, helping them all with his good advice.

AUTHOR'S NOTE

This version of the "Puss in Boots" story—which most likely arrived with colonists from Spain—is well known throughout the Philippines. In most western European tellings (Charles Perrault's 1697 *Le Chat Botté* is the most famous), the clever animal is a cat. In eastern Europe, Siberia, and Mongolia, it is a fox. Some scholars have suggested that all versions of this story may have their origin in much older tales from India about a resourceful jackal.

I have based this retelling largely on four variants in Dean S. Fansler's *Popular Filipino Tales*, published in 1921 as Volume XII of the memoirs of the American Folklore Society. I composited elements from all four and have enhanced the narrative with details from parallel tales cited in Maximo D. Ramos's 1971 *Creatures of Philippine Lower Mythology*.

I also consulted a variety of works on Filipino life and literature and gained added information from discussions with the reference librarians at the public library in Daly City, near San Francisco, which serves one of the largest Filipino communities in California.